Please return/renew this item by the
last date shown to avoid a charge.
Books may also be renewed by phone
and Internet. May not be renewed if
required by another reader.

BARNET
LONDON BOROUGH

For Gözde, who always has a sunshine smile

First published in 2014 in Great Britain by
Barrington Stoke Ltd
18 Walker Street, Edinburgh, EH3 7LP

www.barringtonstoke.co.uk

Text © 2014 Karen McCombie
Illustrations © 2014 Cathy Brett

The moral right of Karen McCombie and Cathy Brett to be identified
as the author and illustrator of this work has been asserted in
accordance with the Copyright, Designs and Patents Act, 1988

A CIP catalogue record for this book is available
from the British Library upon request

ISBN: 978-1-78112-403-1

Printed in China by Leo

Contents

1   Bad to Be Good?   1

2   Will They, Won't They?   5

3   Next, Please!   11

4   I Spy   16

5   What a Welcome (not)   23

6   Please, No!   32

7   Moving-in Day   35

8   *Very* Funny   39

9   The Worst Photo Ever   44

10   So Cool?   50

11   The Opposite of OK   55

12   Hard to Be Happy   58

13   One Year Later   62

Chapter 1

Bad to Be Good?

I have a secret.

A secret *talent*.

I don't ever speak about it – well, only to my best friend Bex.

If I told anyone else, I'd sound like I was a total show-off. A girl with a head the size of a planet. I'd sound like I was all, "Look at me! Look at me!"

That's because my talent is looking ... nice.

What I mean is, I'm good at looking pretty in photos. *And* I'm good at smiling.

See?

That makes me sound bad, doesn't it?

But my nice smile – and the fact that I look pretty in photos – is really important to my family. My family of me and Mum.

When my dad left, he just walked out the door and didn't look back. He didn't come to visit us. He didn't send any money. I was only a toddler, and Mum had to get a job, *fast*.

Mum's special talent is sewing. She set up her own business, making dresses for bridesmaids and flower girls. Work was slow at first, but that changed when Mum got a stall at a wedding fair. She had to take me with her, and I played while grown-ups wandered around and looked at fancy things they could buy for their Big Days.

While we were at the fair, a woman at the next stall gave Mum some advice.

1) Get a website.

2) Post photos of a cute child on it, modelling the dresses.

3) Use *me* as the model, cos of what the woman called my "sunshine smile"!

Mum took the woman's advice.

She dressed me up, put flowers in my hair, posies in my hands and – *snap!* – took my picture.

I was nearly 3 then and I'm 12 now, and I *still* model for her. At weekends, we go to lots of wedding fairs in posh hotels, where they call me "the girl with the sunshine smile".

We're at one of those posh hotels today, and Mum is looking me up and down, to check I'm perfect.

"Hey, do you want our customers to see what you had for breakfast, Meg?" Mum asks me.

I peek in the mirror and grin. Sunshine smiles don't look so good when you have toast crumbs in your teeth!

Chapter 2

Will They, Won't They?

The woman stares at me in a totally dreamy way. OK, so she stares at my *dress*.

"Ooo ..." she murmurs.

The dress is made of white linen, with a buttercup yellow sash around the waist.

"Here, take a leaflet," Mum says, but the woman is lost in wedding daydreams.

"Thanks," the man with her says. He grins at Mum, and looks at the front of the leaflet. "*The Sunshine Dress Company*," he reads out loud. "Do you do any in my size?"

That's pretty funny and Mum giggles. It's not just funny cos he's a man. It's cos he's a very *messy* man. Most of the boyfriends here at the wedding fair are clean and tidy. They have combed their hair and shaved. They're wearing nice shirts and smart jeans.

This man has messy stubble, dark red hair that sticks up at all angles, and jeans that are covered in smears of black grease.

I take a step away from him, scared the grease will somehow leap from his jeans and onto my dress if he gets too close.

"Hey, Danny – can you imagine my little flower girl Alice in this?" the woman says at last.

"Yep," the man says. "She'd look very nice. Unlike my boys, who'll just want to wear their skate shorts."

"They will not!" the woman says. She gives the man a jokey slap on the arm, but she seems a bit cross.

"Your boys aren't keen on getting smart, then?" Mum asks.

"Danny's son Charlie said he'll only come to the wedding if he can bring his skateboard," the woman says. She rolls her eyes.

"My youngest son Leo told me he'll only come if I promise to buy him a pet rat," the man adds. "But I think his brother Frank put him up to that."

"You have *three* sons?" Mum says. "Wow, your house must be noisy!"

I'm thinking the same thing. Me and Mum live in a small, ground-floor flat in a block by the park. Every room is painted cream. I love our peaceful, girly home. It's comfy and quiet.

I can't imagine living with three roaring, loud boys.

"Ha!" the woman snorts. "Danny has *four* sons."

"Four sons, a cat with three legs and a bike repair business," Danny says. He points to the greasy stains on his jeans. "Don't forget about that."

"How could I forget?" the woman says. "And how could you forget that you promised to come with me today?"

Now *she's* pointing at the man's dirty clothes. Seems like he didn't have time to change out of them.

"Aw, come on, Jen! I said sorry, didn't I?" he says, and he leads the woman away from our stall. "Let me buy you a coffee and cake to make up for it ..."

As they go off towards the café, the man gives me and Mum a wave and a smile.

At the same time, Mum asks, "So, Meg. What do you reckon?"

What she means is, what do I reckon this Jen and Danny's chances are? Will they end up married? Will they stay married? It's a bit cheeky, I know, but it's something we have fun with at wedding fairs – we like to guess which couples will last and which won't.

"Zero chance," I say wickedly, even though my smile is still as sweet and bright as sunshine.

Chapter 3

Next, Please!

A few weeks after the wedding fair, I'm back at school and there's a note stuck to the gym door. "Queue here for School Photos," it says.

The gym windows light up from the camera flashes inside.

"I *hate* getting my photo taken!" Bex moans, as we wait in a long line in the playground. She checks her braces and her mass of messy dark curls in a tiny mirror.

"It's OK," I say. I'm happy that we're out in the fresh air instead of stuck in the classroom.

"It's OK for you, Meg!" Bex says, and she passes me the mirror. "You're used to it. You've had your photo taken a gazillion times."

She's right. It's not just Mum who has taken my photo over the years. My picture's been in the local newspaper and even a couple of wedding magazines. It's kind of fun, and I guess I should make the most of it. I'll soon be too big to model Mum's kid-size dresses.

"Hey, Meg, I'm talking to you," Bex says. "Are you OK? You've been lost in your own little world a lot, the last while."

"Have I?" I gaze up from the mirror and frown at Bex. But there's no time to think about what she's just said, because the line of students moves forward.

At last we're in the gym, and Bex is in front of the photographer.

"Smile!" he tells her. "Come on – you can do better than that!"

Bex pushes her tangle of curls from her face, gives a quick, shy grin, and the flash pops.

"Next!"

My turn.

I slide onto the stool where my best friend was just sitting. I look up and smile my best smile, but the photographer's not looking at me.

"Sorry – be with you in a sec," he mutters, as he fiddles with his camera.

That spare second lets me mull over what Bex said.

I suppose I have been less chatty over the last few weeks. Less sunshiny too – at least inside. It's because of Mum, I realise. Me and her have always been close. We've had no choice, since we're a family of two. But the last few weeks, something has been different – it feels like there's a distance between us …

The photographer interrupts my thoughts. "OK, let's have a big smile," he calls out.

FLASH!

In that blinking moment it hits me – Mum is hiding something from me, isn't she?

And – oops – I think I just forgot how to smile.

Chapter 4

I Spy

I am spying on my own mother.

So is my friend Bex.

Together we will find out what it is that Mum is hiding from me.

Bex lives two floors above me in our block of flats, and we're at her bedroom window, peering at the road below.

"Where did she say she was going?" Bex asks, as she passes me a packet of cookies.

"Book club," I tell her. "Again."

I'm no detective, but it just doesn't add up. I haven't seen any new books in our flat. And I'm pretty sure most book clubs only meet once a month. Mum has been getting a babysitter and going out every Saturday for weeks now. But this Saturday I'm having a sleepover here at Bex's. Bex's big sister is away on a school trip, so I'm in her bunk in the bedroom they share.

"Look – there's your mum!" Bex says. She points with one hand and brushes cookie crumbs off her checked shirt with the other.

Yep, it's Mum, wearing her favourite deep purple dress and cool ankle boots.

Bex and I look at each other – we're both thinking the same thing. My mum doesn't look like she's going to a book club, not one bit. And then Bex asks, "Hey, who's *that*?"

We both watch as Mum waves to a man on the other side of the street. He waves back, then he crosses the road, puts his arm round Mum and they stroll off together.

I stare at them in shock. "I don't know," I tell Bex.

But then I notice the man's dark red hair and all of a sudden I remember ...

He's the man with the bike grease on his jeans and the cross girlfriend. From the wedding fair. The man and woman I decided had zero chance of staying together.

Mum is dating *him* ...? Mum is dating someone else's husband-to-be. How could she? How dare she?

***

"Hello, darling!" Mum says, as I walk back into our flat the next morning. She's at her sewing machine, which is covered in a mountain of

white linen and strips of rose-pink ribbon. "Did you have fun at Bex's?"

I ignore her. It's no good acting as if everything is OK. How can everything be OK when my own mother has a secret boyfriend?

Someone else's boyfriend!

I decide to be blunt. "Do you want to tell me what's going on?" I ask.

"What do you mean, Meg?" Mum says.

She's still acting, but I spot that her cheeks are flushed as pink as the ribbon she's sewing.

"Please don't pretend you're in a book club," I say, and I pull my best "don't-lie-to-me" face. "Danny – that's his name, isn't it?" I ask. I'm daring her to deny it.

Mum gasps. "It's not what you think," she blurts out.

I go silent. I'm not going to make this easy for her. Not when she's been keeping secrets. *Bad* secrets.

"Danny phoned me about a week after that wedding fair and asked me out," she says. "I was taken aback – till he explained. Jen, the woman he was with that day … she's his sister, not his girlfriend."

It takes a minute for the truth to sink in.

"OK," I say at last, in a hurt voice. "But why have you kept this hidden from me?"

"Oh, Meg," Mum says, and she comes out from behind the sewing machine. I think she wants to give me a hug, but she's scared I'll stomp off. "We had to be sure how we felt about each other," she tells me. "Before I told you it was for real, I mean."

For real. *That* sounds serious.

"In fact, I was going to tell you today," Mum carries on, "because Danny has invited us for tea. Is that OK?"

Mum bites her lip and waits for me to speak.

She wants me to say yes. She wants a sunshine smile.

But I'm not in the mood to play along with her. Anyway, what is there to smile about? It's always been just me and Mum, best friends as well as mother and daughter. But all of a sudden, everything has changed. Big time.

Chapter 5

What a Welcome (not)

Four boys stare at me. One is a teenager, one is a little kid, and two are in between. The littlest one is picking his nose.

I feel sick.

Not because of nerves or the nose-picking. (Gross!) I feel sick because Danny and his four staring sons live on a boat.

OK, a barge.

Their home is a giant hunk of wood floating on the river, on the not-very-pretty side near the big supermarket. It's called "Bluebell" and is surrounded by lots more boats and barges. Mum and me got onto it by walking along wobbly gangways from the jetty. And the simple fact that I'm standing here on the open top deck is making me feel like I'm about to vomit.

"Well, who is going to give Meg a tour of 'Bluebell'?" Danny asks his sons in a too-cheerful voice. As he speaks he "tidies" some bits of bike away by kicking them towards a mismatched garden table and chairs.

"Not me!" a boy with dark hair yells. I've been told this is Frank. He's 8.

"Not me too!" yells another boy who is like Frank's mini-me. This is 4-year-old Leo.

Then they both run off sniggering.

Danny gives Mum a look that I'm sure means, "Sorry about my boys!"

"What about you?" Danny says to a tall, lanky boy. He must be Charlie. He is 14, the oldest of Danny's sons.

"Got to take this call!" Charlie says – even though his mobile hasn't even rung.

"Well, Seb – that leaves you," Danny says. He nods at the last boy, who is 12, same as me.

"Ughhh," Seb sighs, and he rubs a hand through a mop of spiky hair that's the same dark red as his dad's. "Do I *have* to?"

"Seb!" his dad says, with a shocked laugh.

"OK, OK," Seb grumbles. He waves at me to follow him down an open hatch.

"Go on, Meg," Mum says. "This place is so amazing! You'll love it!"

"I don't think I will," I mutter to myself, as I take careful steps backwards down the ladder.

My tummy churns and my head swirls as the seasick feeling washes over me again.

"So you just saw the deck, where we eat if the weather is OK, and where Dad works," Seb says. He sounds bored. "And this ... this is the living room and the kitchen."

As my feet touch the floor, I turn and look. The barge inside reminds me of a caravan. Bench-style seats line the walls. There is a built-in cupboard with a tiny telly stuck on top. Tatty, short curtains hang on droopy wires at the windows.

This place would look cute if it was tidy, which it's not.

I have never seen so much boy mess. Trainers, jumpers, bags are everywhere. I kick away a grungy stray sock with the toe of my ballet pump. (Yuck.)

This is my first visit, but Mum told me that she has been here a few times. How can she stand it? Our flat is like a palace compared to this scuzzy pig pen.

"Dad's bedroom is through the back," Seb says. He doesn't even bother to look at me. "Ours are on the bottom level."

"Is that where your bathroom is too?" I ask, feeling woozy again.

"Uh-huh," Seb mutters, and he nods to another hatch.

"I can manage," I tell him, as I hurry over to the top of a set of steep steps. I don't need his company for this – especially if I really am going to be sick.

"Please yourself," he says with a don't-care shrug.

In the bathroom, I splash cold water on my face in the weeny sink. I feel better instantly. And, while I'm here, I decide I'll try to have a wee – just so I don't have to do the ladders again later. I sit down on the loo, and I think of what Mum told me this morning – that Danny and his sons moved to the barge after the boys' mum died. Leo was only a baby back then and Danny had to work part-time to look after him, so he sold their "normal" house and bought this barge, which was much cheaper.

"Danny knew it was right when he saw the boat's name," Mum said on the way here. "Bluebells were his wife's favourite flower …"

It's a really sweet, sad story.

But you can tell no woman has ever lived here, that's for sure. I mean, no sensible woman would put up with having no lock on the bathroom door. (I shoved the washing basket against it to keep it closed.)

THUD!

Uh-oh.

The door swings open. The washing basket spills socks and pants like dirty cloth confetti all over the floor. Frank is standing there, staring at me.

Me with my jeans around my ankles ...

"Ha ha ha ha ha!" he yelps, then runs away.

He's going to tell his brothers about this, isn't he?

And I'm going to tell Mum that I'm never, ever visiting "Bluebell" again, no matter how sad and sweet Danny's story is.

Chapter 6

Please, No!

I'm trying to look happy, for the sake of all the couples who are strolling past Mum's stall, but it's not working. After the total *shame* of what happened on the barge I have lost my sunshine smile.

I glance around for Mum, but I see she's still outside. It's Sunday and she's trying to get hold of our landlord, cos there's been a bit of a disaster at home.

While Mum is busy, I sneak a call of my own. It isn't very classy to use a mobile when you're modelling a pretty bridesmaid's dress, but I need to speak to Bex.

"Hey, you!" I say, as soon as she picks up.

"Hey, you!" she says back. "Feeling better?"

She means the loo disaster of course. I will never feel better about that.

"Worse!" I tell her. "We had a flood in our flat today. A pipe burst – and the plumber has no idea why!"

"Really?" Bex gasps. "That sounds bad, Meg!"

"It is. The place is a *mess*. I hope it's easy to fix, cos Mum cracked a joke just now that made me feel ill."

"Yeah?" Bex says. "What was that?"

"She said that if the flat needs lots of work, then maybe we'll have to go and stay on Danny's barge."

"Ha!" Bex snorts. I can picture her dark curls bouncing as she laughs.

"Can you imagine?" I say. "Me on that barge. With all those *boys*!"

Then I spot Mum coming back to the stall.

"Got to go, Bex," I say. I switch my mobile off and hide it behind my back.

I'm feeling giggly after talking to my best friend. But that feeling fades pretty fast when I see Mum's face.

She looks hassled. Like she has news she doesn't want to tell me. Bad news.

Please, no ... *not* the barge!

Chapter 7

Moving-in Day

Most people don't take sea-sickness pills when they move house, do they?

But I've taken one. The rocking of Danny's barge really gets to me. And I reckon I'll have to take one every day that we're staying here. Mum says that's going to be at least one week. Maybe two.

It's just my luck. My *bad* luck, I mean.

Why did the broken pipe have to be such a major problem? Why did it have to mean that workmen in big boots needed to come and stomp around our neat flat?

I tried hard not to come here today.
I don't want to be on this scruffy, crowded,
always-moving barge. I begged Bex to let me
stay at hers, but her sister is back from her
school trip and there's no room.

So here I am, standing with my wheelie
suitcase on the swaying gangway. Charlie is
passing Mum's stuff up to Seb, while Danny
helps Mum across the big gap between the
gangway and the barge.

It's my turn.

"Don't fall in!" Frank yells. Leo giggles.

"Here," Danny says.

I ignore his offer of a hand to hold – then
I feel scared when I see the sloshing muddy
water below me and I give a little yelp.

"Ha ha ha!" Frank and Leo laugh.

"Don't mind them, Meg," Danny says, with a nod to his sons. "And don't look down!"

This time I take both his hands and get myself on deck.

Next, Danny shows me to the cabin that is mine for now.

When he goes, I look around.

It's small as a wardrobe and smells of dust and damp. There's a tiny bed and a bare rail to hang my clothes on, and that's it – apart from a mirror that hangs lop-sided on the wall. I try to shift it but it just tilts again, cos the barge is tilted. ("That happens at low tide," Mum told me.)

My face in the lop-sided mirror looks like thunder. How am I going to survive this week? Maybe I'll just lock myself away in this tiny room. Stay away from those boys, and –

"Aaaaarghh!!"

I can't help yelping again – a low-down panel in the wall has moved and something has burst in. Hold on …

It's two somethings. Frank and Leo!

Now I remember what else Mum told me. On the barge, all the rooms connect like this, to make escape hatches in case of a fire.

"Boo!" the boys yell. "Ha ha ha!"

I've only been here five minutes and already it's a nightmare.

Get me out of here!

Chapter 8

Very Funny

Squint.

It's a funny word but it is perfect to describe my life.

Thanks to the low tide, the barge was squint again this morning. That meant I woke up by rolling right out of bed. (Ouch.)

Mum made me an omelette for breakfast, which was cooked in a squint way – thicker on one side than the other.

Then I had a squint bath, with all the water up one end.

I looked at myself in the squint mirror in my cabin – then screamed when something squint jumped in the open porthole window. (It was Tigger, Danny and the boys' 3-legged cat.)

To Charlie, Seb, Frank and Leo this was all *very* funny.

They didn't think it was so funny when I stomped off to dry my hair. I used my new, powerful hairdryer – and all the lights in the barge went out!

As the boys groaned, Danny explained that the barge has a weak electricity supply. How crazy is that? What am I supposed to do? Go to school with wet hair all week?

"Have a nice day," Mum says, and she passes me my schoolbag.

I pass her the towel I rubbed my hair dry with.

I can't look at her. She wants me to be happy – she wants this to work out. But I'm damp and grumpy.

I'm even more grumpy when I go up the steps to the deck and hear Leo giggle. "I can see up your skirt, Meg!" he says.

With a jump, I land on the gangway and hurry away from the barge, and the four horrible boys on it.

But it's hard to hurry. My legs feel like jelly.

"Got land legs?" a voice says.

It's Charlie. He grins and nods down towards my feet.

I don't grin back. "What do you mean?" I snap.

"It's what you call it when you're not used to boats," he says. "It feels like the ground is made of marshmallow, right?"

Marshmallow sounds sweet, but Charlie and his brothers are not sweet. In fact, they're as far from sweet as it's possible to be.

With all their digs and sniggers, I can tell Danny's sons are enjoying my stay about as much as I am.

Which is not at all.

Chapter 9

The Worst Photo Ever

I have stayed on the barge for three long days now.

It's been hard.

I have hidden away in my cabin a lot – doing my homework, reading, listening to music. (My wheelie case is wedged against the escape hatch door.)

Bex has been brilliant. Today she took me back to her place for a real treat – a non-squint bath in a boy-free flat. It was total luxury. I lay there for ages and listened to the playlist blasting out from her room. (Bex chose all my favourite tracks.) And, after my bath, I spent a long, long, *long* time blow-drying my hair without the power going off.

Bex's mum asked me to stay for tea, but – get this – my mum said no!

When I called her, she told me I had to come back to the barge. She and Danny had made something special for tea.

Whoop-dee-doo!

It could be a fancy meal fit for royalty, but I'd rather share a bowl of crunchies with Tigger the 3-legged cat than sit and eat with Danny's four annoying sons.

But here I am, mooching along the gangway as slowly as I can. I don't care if I'm late. In fact, I stop and stare at the view for a while.

It's a warm evening and the river bank on the other side is lovely. The pink glow of the setting sun ripples in the water. Across from the boats, people stroll along with friends and dogs. For a second I feel almost happy – till I remember where I have to be. And who with (sadly) …

I sigh and stomp onwards, then stop dead.

"Bluebell" is *twinkling*.

Ropes of soft white fairy lights are strung back and forth above the deck. I recognise those fairy lights – Mum sells them on her stall for weddings. It's kind of funny to see them here on this scuzzy boat. They make it seem almost magical.

"Mum?" I call out as I clamber on board.

"Do you like it, Meg?" she asks. She sounds shy and hopeful.

"It looks good," I say. "Pretty." Then I notice an odd thing. My heart lurches a bit – it feels like the boat rocking in the river. Leo is holding Mum's hand. I'm not sure how that makes me feel.

"Hey, Meg!" Danny calls. "Can you take this?"

His head is peeking out from the hatch on deck, and he's holding a tray of food.

"Sure," I reply.

I drop my schoolbag on the deck and it flops to one side. Some of my stuff tumbles out, but I'll sort it in a sec – I need to help Danny.

"Wow," I say, when I put the tray down on the table. There's tons of food and it all looks great.

"Daddy's been cooking all day," Leo says. "And I put the flowers in the vase!"

I smile at the clump of dandelions bunched in a jam jar.

I feel myself relax here for the very first time. Maybe a few more days on "Bluebell" won't hurt, after all.

"Ha ha ha ha!"

That sounds like Frank.

"Nice picture – not!" Seb cackles.

I spin around and see what has fallen out of my bag to be snatched up by the boys. "Give me that!" I snap.

It's my school photo – the one that was taken when I realised Mum had a secret she was keeping from me. It's the worst photo of me *ever*. My mouth is hanging open and I look stunned, like I've had an electric shock.

I grab the photo from Seb and chuck it over the side of the barge. I hope it sinks to the bottom of the river.

If only I could do the same to Seb and Frank.

I wish.

Chapter 10

So Cool?

"Popcorn?" Bex asks me.

It's Friday and it's movie night. Not at the local cinema, but on the deck of a barge which belongs to one of Danny's neighbours.

A screen on a stand flaps gently in the breeze. Little kids are kicking cushions into wiggly rows for people to sit on once the sun sets and the film starts. Some teenagers are handing out popcorn in chipped mugs.

"No thanks," I say to Bex, who is here to keep me company. And to listen to my moans. (I've just found out that we have to stay *another* week.)

"Watching a film outdoors on a river ..." Bex murmurs. "It's so cool, Meg!"

Cool? I don't think so. It's mad!

"How often does it happen?" she asks.

"Um, Danny says every couple of weeks in the summer," I reply.

"Yeah?" Bex says. "I'm so jealous. I want to live here!"

Huh? This whole place is *weird*. Having a boat as a home is *weird*. Anyone who wants to do that is *weird*.

"So where are Danny's sons?" Bex asks. She twirls a curl in her fingers and gazes around at all the boys and girls – some on the deck, some on the river bank – who are chatting, laughing and fooling around.

"The tall boy over there is Charlie," I say. Charlie's one of the popcorn waiters, handing out mugs. "And that one is Seb." Seb is helping his dad move a table.

"Oh, *he's* cute!" Bex says.

No! I don't want her to think that! What next? Will she say that Frank and Leo are adorable? Who knows where they are, but –

"RAARGGGHHH!"

The loud roar makes me jump, and the thud on my back takes me by surprise.

I slip to one side, my balance gone. I lurch and stumble and reach for Bex, but I miss her and clutch at thin air instead.

Then all of a sudden I tip over the handrail, falling fast.

A whoosh of air.

A yell for help.

Then the cold water takes my breath away.

Chapter 11

The Opposite of OK

I'm in water again, but at least this time it's hot. And bubbly.

"Meg?" Mum calls from the other side of the bathroom door. "Are you OK?"

How can I be OK? I fell into a river. All because Frank was showing Leo some so-called "deadly ninja moves" and the little weasel crashed into me.

"Meg?" Mum calls again. "Can I come in?"

Of course she can come in. There's no lock on the stupid door of this stupid bathroom on this stupid boat.

I don't reply, but Mum comes in anyway and sits on the edge of the bath.

"Frank really is *very* sorry," she says, and strokes my hair. (It still smells of muddy water, even after I've shampooed it twice.)

I shrug. All I can think of is how scary it was in the water. I'll never forget that feeling of going under. When I got to the surface I spluttered for breath and grabbed the life ring that Charlie threw to me. And then Danny and Seb pulled me up to safety, with all those faces staring. Oh, the *shame* ...

"He's made this for you," Mum says.

She holds out a piece of paper folded in half. It says "SORRY!" in big letters, in all different colours. She opens it for me. "And Leo drew this."

Inside is a wonky picture of something that looks like a fish in a wig.

"It's you, Meg," Mum says, with a little smile. "As a mermaid!"

Mum may be smiling, but I'm not.

It doesn't matter how cute the boys are. The "sorry" card and the fish-in-a-wig drawing won't make me change my mind.

I can't stand it here and I am *not* staying.

Chapter 12

Hard to Be Happy

I'm not in the mood to be wearing this bridesmaid's dress.

"Meg, you're frowning again," Mum teases me. "You'll scare my customers away. Stop it!"

Well, that's easy for her to say, but it's hard to be happy.

Smiling couples are all around me at today's wedding fair. They don't have a clue that last night I got dunked in a river. That my mum got upset when I told her I was leaving. That I slept at my best friend's.

"Look, I'm going to phone the landlord again," Mum says. "We'll see if we can get back to the flat any sooner. OK?"

I give her a "yes please" nod. At least she's trying to make things better. I really hope we can move back in – I have a sore neck from sleeping on Bex's hard bedroom floor, and a big bruise on my arm where Bex's sister jumped down from her bunk and stood on me by mistake.

Mum drifts out of the crowded hall to make her call … and I realise someone is talking to me.

"Excuse me – hello?" It's a little kid, tugging at my dress. That's not good – I can't get dirty fingerprints on this! I go to tug it free, and then I see that the little kid is Leo.

"Meg, *please* don't be angry with us!" he says, and he holds out a tatty bunch of dandelions.

59

I feel the frown fall from my face. It's the cutest thing ever.

"Thank you, Leo," I say. I take the dandelions and sniff them as if they smell lovely, and not like cat wee.

"We're all really sorry," I hear a man's voice say. "Please can we start again?"

I look up and see Danny, with Charlie, Seb and Frank. The three bigger boys look shy and sorry, instead of sneery.

I try to smile, but I think I've forgotten how to.

Is it too late?

For me to get the sunshine back in my smile, *and* for us all to get along?

Chapter 13

One Year Later

The twinkling ropes of fairy lights sway in the evening breeze.

The blue sky is streaked pink and peach as the sun sets. It's warm, and the crowd of people on the top deck of Danny's barge are in a party mood.

I'm watching it all from a chair tucked in the prow of the boat, where it's shadier.

"What *is* he doing?" Bex asks from beside me. She's just spotted Frank. He's dragging a bunch of silver balloons behind him as he runs around the deck. The balloons are bashing all the dancers in his way.

"Leo says it's an experiment," I tell her. "Frank's trying to catch Tigger and tie the balloons to her collar."

"To make Tigger fly," Leo adds. He's sitting on my lap and sounds sleepy. It's been a long day for a little boy.

"Good luck with that!" Bex says, with a grin. "Hey, I haven't seen your mum for a bit. Where is she?"

"Over there, talking to Jen," I say, and I point at Mum and Danny's sister, who are chatting by the scruffy old table that Mum's painted sky blue and silver. Jen is admiring the beautiful cake sitting in the middle of it.

"Your mum looks so lovely!" Bex sighs.

It's true – Mum looks amazing.

She's wearing a floaty shirt with a pattern of birds, cut-off denim shorts and flip-flops with jewels on them. My outfit is kind of the same, but I'm wearing this cool vest top with a rainbow on it.

Leo points to the flower in Mum's hair. "Snap!" he says with a giggle, and he reaches up to touch the pink velvet rose holding one side of my hair back.

"Mum wanted us to match," I whisper to Leo, and I give him a cuddle. "I am her bridesmaid, after all!"

"I'm going to have a wedding like this when I'm older!" Bex announces with a grin. She spins around in her party outfit – a T-shirt dress with a sequinned skull and crossbones on the front.

I think Mum's plan for her own wedding surprised all the wedding fair stall-holders. But after so many years of making fancy clothes, she wanted something simple for herself. And Danny and the boys were very happy about that. They're all in baggy shorts and Hawaiian shirts.

"Want to dance?" I hear Seb ask.

I look around. Luckily, he's not asking me, since Leo is nodding off in my arms.

"Sure!" says a blushing Bex. She goes off to join the whooping dancers and spin some more. Charlie is doing a great job as DJ.

As I watch Bex and Seb dance, I spot Danny trying to catch my eye. "OK?" he mouths at me from across the deck.

"Yes!" I mouth back.

I am more than OK. It's funny to think that a year ago, I didn't much like Danny's barge. And I thought I had zero chance of ever getting along with his sons.

But now I can't imagine a time when I didn't know them – "Bluebell" *and* the boys!

I gaze around at the dancing party guests, at the twinkling fairy lights, at Danny hugging my laughing mum, at Frank and Tigger zig-zagging through the crowd.

Then I look down at my new little brother and see that Leo is fast asleep, with one hand around my neck.

Suddenly I realise that I have never been so happy.

There is no camera around to snap me.

But, in the twilight, I smile my brightest ever sunshine smile ...

Our books are tested
for children and young people by
children and young people.

Thanks to everyone who consulted on
a manuscript for their time and effort in
helping us to make our books better
for our readers.